For Hayley and Fraser,
with lots of love.

Sorry it took so long!

PARTY POOPERS

JILL YOUNG

Illustrated by Samantha Webb

CONTENTS

1. POTION MAKERS

'Ta-dah!' sang Lauren, 'our potion factory!'

'Isn't that the summer house?' Eve was confused.

'Not now Mum's got her shiny new decking and super-duper extending gazebo. This is all ours!' announced Lauren's twin brother Jamie. 'Wait until you see inside.'

'Wow!' Eve was impressed. The twins had pushed the chairs to the back of the room so they could all sit on the floor around the coffee table. The ingredients they had been collecting for their potions were arranged in various tubs and jars along the window sill. 'I brought some more pots,' Eve said, producing them from her bag, 'and...' she paused for dramatic effect, '...I've got these!' She laid a handful of tiny bottles on the table.

'Wow! Cool! What are they?' asked Jamie.

'They're little samples of perfume my mum gave me. I thought they'd make the potions smell nice.'

'Brilliant! Let me smell them.' Lauren reached for the bottles as Jamie groaned in exasperation.

'Never mind what they smell like. We need to make them work first.'

Just then there was a shout from the house. 'Jamie! Alfie's here. I'll just send him down.'

'Oh no, we need to hide all this stuff. Alfie doesn't know about the potions.' Jamie started gathering everything into a pile just as their friend arrived at the door of the summer house.

'Hey guys, what's going on?' Alfie asked.

'Nothing,' the other three all spoke at the same time, trying really hard not to look like they were hiding something.

'What are you hiding?' Alfie tried again. 'What's all that stuff for?'

'Nothing, just stuff.'

'Doesn't look like nothing. What are you doing with it? Can I play?'

Lauren and Eve both looked at Jamie who shrugged. 'We're making potions,' Lauren explained.

'What, magic potions?' Alfie looked

impressed.

'Well that was the plan, but we're having a bit of trouble with the magic part.' Eve explained how they had been collecting petals and leaves from some of the plants in the garden and mixing them up with sand and water and lots of other bits and pieces to try to create the perfect potion. She showed him their latest creation which was a lovely shade of blue thanks to some bubble mixture they had added. There were a few small leaves floating on top. Alfie looked impressed until Jamie had to admit that, technically, it wasn't really a potion because it didn't do anything.

Lauren put the lid back on the blue mixture before putting it in her pocket. 'Let's go and get an ice pole and try to come up with some new ideas,' she said to the others, leading the way back to the house.

The four friends took their ice poles to the playground down the street and crawled into the den under the bushes. They were all so busy eating and trying to decide what to do next that they didn't notice two boys from their class pushing their way through to the den. Sam and Charlie weren't usually very kind to their classmates and today was no different.

'Oh look, a bunch of babies hiding in the bushes,' sneered Charlie. 'What have you got today, babies?'

'Go away Charlie and leave us alone,' said Lauren.

'Ooh that's not very nice, Baby Lauren. Did you hear that Sam? Baby Lauren wants us to go away.'

Sam laughed but didn't say anything. He was sometimes quite nice at school but he was always horrible when he was with Charlie.

Charlie spotted the potion which Jamie was now holding. 'What have you got there, Baby Jamie? Is that your baby food?' Charlie tried to take the tub but Jamie snatched it away.

'It's none of your business,' Jamie growled, knowing that Charlie would make fun of them if he found out about the potions.

'That's not very friendly, Baby Jamie.' Charlie turned to his friend and laughed. 'Definitely some kind of baby food, Sam.'

'If you must know, it's a magic potion that turns mean people like you to ice,' Jamie blurted out. His three friends looked at him in horror. They were all used to Charlie being spiteful and they all knew the best thing to do was not say anything that might make it worse. Jamie had just made it worse – much worse. Charlie burst out laughing.

'A magic potion? Do you really expect us to believe that? Watch out Sam, they're going to freeze us!' The two boys laughed together, annoying Jamie even more.

'Go away and leave us alone or I'll have no choice. I'll have to use it on you. Then you'll see,' he warned. Eve and Lauren looked at each other. *See what?* They were both wondering.

'Oh please,' laughed Charlie, 'gimme your best shot!'

'OK, but don't say I didn't warn you.' He slowly stirred the blue mixture with his finger, playing for time as he tried desperately to work out what to do next. He really needed help from his friends right now, or even his sister, but they all seemed to be trying to make themselves invisible.

'How come your finger isn't freezing?' challenged Charlie.

Jamie thought fast. 'The potion isn't complete yet,' he explained. 'I need to add the key ingredient.' He looked over at the others hoping that one of them had come up with something but it was clear from their faces that wasn't going to happen. None of them knew how they were going to get out of this situation without looking very stupid. Once that happened, Charlie and Sam were sure to tell the whole school and everyone would laugh at them.

'Get on with it then,' urged Charlie, 'I'm bored with all this waiting.'

Jamie very slowly and carefully broke off

a small piece of ice pole and added it to the mixture, swirling the pot gently. He had given up hoping for any help from the others and kept his eyes firmly fixed on the potion, hoping no-one would see the tears starting to form. He still didn't have a plan but he knew he was going to have to get on with it even if it meant Charlie making a fool of him for the rest of his life.

'Hold out your hand.'

Charlie did as he was asked, grinning from ear to ear because he knew there was no magic in the pot.

'I'm going to count to three then pour the liquid over your hand. Are you sure you want me to do this?' Jamie asked, using his best delaying tactics. 'It's not too late to change your mind.'

'Get on with it,' snapped Charlie. 'I can't

believe you're going through all this. We both know perfectly well that you're just going to end up proving how stupid you really are.'

Jamie had completely run out of ideas. He looked at Lauren hoping for a last-minute reprieve. Lauren looked at Eve. Eve looked at Alfie. Alfie looked like he wished he'd never asked to help with all this potions nonsense.

There was nothing else for it.

'OK, here we go…one…two…'

'Aaagghh! Spider!' Alfie screamed, jumping up and knocking the potion right out of Jamie's hand. All six children watched the pot as it flew through the air, the blue liquid spraying out behind it like the tail of a kite.

'You have got to be kidding me,' said Charlie. 'Is that really the best you could do?

You tell us all this rubbish about a magic potion then, whoopsie, it accidentally gets spilt before you can prove that it works.' Charlie glowered at Jamie, shaking his head in disbelief. He was about to say something else when his friend interrupted.

'Er, Charlie,' said Sam gripping his friend's arm, 'look!' Sam was pointing to the leaves and the branch the potion had landed on. 'They're frozen solid,' he whispered.

'No way,' Charlie couldn't believe his eyes but, when he pulled one of the leaves, it snapped off in his hands. 'No way,' he repeated, grabbing another leaf, absolutely gobsmacked by what he was seeing. He turned and stared at Jamie, fixing his eyes on him as he backed out of the den. Sam was right behind him. As soon as they were clear of the trees, they both ran off as fast as they

could across the park.

The four friends looked at the icy patch in amazement.

'How on earth did you do that?' Eve asked, turning to Jamie.

'I have absolutely no idea,' he replied.

'It's amazing what you can do if you just believe in yourself.'

'What?'

'What do you mean, what?'

'I mean what did you just say?'

'I didn't say anything.'

'Yes, you did. You said something was amazing.'

'No, I didn't!'

'So, who did?' Jamie looked at Eve and Alfie who both shrugged.

'Me!' called a very small voice. 'I'm up here!'

The four children looked up to see a tiny little man, dressed completely in pink, sitting on a branch above their heads.

2. PROFESSOR MIXER

The children stared in silence as the little pink man climbed down to stand in front of them. He was very smart in his slim, pin-striped trousers, waistcoat and cravat. With a pair of sunglasses pushed up onto the top of his head and fabulous pointy-toed, snake-skin boots, he looked like a miniature rock star. Only, most rock stars weren't completely pink. The little man gave a deep bow, sweeping his arm wide from left to right as he did so. 'Professor Mixer at your service…but you can call me Neville.'

None of the children knew what to say. Things were turning so strange, Lauren actually wondered if she'd fallen down a rabbit hole, like Alice in Wonderland. Her brother had apparently invented a freezing potion and now they were talking to a little pink man. Well, he was talking to them, but it was still strange.

As usual, it was Eve that found her voice first, although a much smaller version than usual. 'Pleased to meet you, Neville, I'm Eve,' she whispered.

'Oh, I know who you are – all of you. I've been keeping a very close watch on you over the past few days. I knew you were getting close with your potion recipe and I didn't want you to slip through the net, if you know what I mean.' Neville chuckled to himself but the children didn't know what he meant. Where was this net he was talking about and why did he want them in it? The four friends moved closer together. They all knew they weren't supposed to talk to strangers but this little man was no bigger than Alfie's cat. Besides, they were all desperate to know why he'd been watching them. Eve asked him to explain.

'It's quite simple really,' Neville said. 'I work for the Professional Organisation of Outstanding Potioneers or POOP as we like to call it.' The children giggled but Neville continued. 'I am very sad to say that POOP is struggling. Our numbers are reducing every year.' He paused for dramatic effect. 'Those of us who remain at POOP are trying very hard to recruit new members but it would seem that potioneering is a dying art. I

haven't had so much as a sniff of a new POOPer for many a month until I stumbled upon your factory last week. I almost wept when I realised what you were doing and how good your recipe was. You are just the sort of people we need to keep POOP going!'

Jamie was confused. 'But we didn't even think the potion was ready. We certainly didn't think it would work. That's why Alfie knocked it out of my hand. He was trying to make us look less stupid.'

'Exactly!' exclaimed Neville. 'Each and every one of you was wishing so hard that it would work and, let's face it, it's time those horrible boys learned a lesson. Well done for directing the potion away from them though, Alfie. I would have been powerless to help if it had actually touched them.'

'You mean you made the potion work?'

asked Lauren, 'not Jamie?'

'I might have helped just a little bit,' Neville admitted. 'It was only temporary though. If you check the grass now, you'll see it's all defrosted. You're so close to getting things right. I just didn't want you to be disheartened.'

'So, what do we need to do to get it right?' asked Jamie.

'Hmm…well…that's where things get a bit awkward,' Neville stroked his beard as he spoke. 'I'm not actually allowed to tell you that. You have to work it out for yourselves. It's the main rule of POOP!' he cried as the children started to protest. 'We have to make sure that anyone allowed to be a POOPer has shown the necessary skills and initiative required of a great potioneer. I shouldn't even have visited you until you proved that your potions work but, as I said, you're so close. I really thought that, if you'd failed this time, you would just have given up.'

'We would,' the girls said together.

'No, we wouldn't,' argued Jamie, 'we're never giving up.'

'Let's face it Jamie, if that hadn't worked, you and I would have been laughed out of town. We would have had no choice but to give up,' said Alfie.

'Whatever,' huffed Jamie. 'Anyway, it did work. Now all we need to do is work out how to make it work again.'

'That's the spirit!' Neville was pleased. 'And you need to remember that the most important thing you have is each other. Four brains are far better than one so make sure you use them all. Anyway, I must be off but I'll be keeping an eye on you. For now, I need to go and enrol you all as Practice POOPers.'

'Excuse me?' Eve had absolutely no desire to become any kind of POOPer, never mind a practice one.

'When you first join us, you're known as a Practice POOPer,' Neville explained. 'Once you pass your probationary period, you become a Party POOPer,' he giggled, 'I thought of that one, do you like it?' The children stared at him blankly. 'Oh well, never mind, if you work really hard you can shake that one off pretty quickly and be promoted to a Premier POOPer, like me. Good luck!' and he took off back up the tree, swinging from branch to branch until he disappeared from sight.

The children stared after Neville for a while until they eventually realised that he wasn't coming back.

'Could somebody pinch me please,' asked Alfie. 'I just had a dream about a little pink guy that wanted me to become a POOPer.'

'That wasn't a dream,' Lauren said, 'it actually happened.'

Alfie made a strange groaning noise. 'I SO didn't want you to say that.'

3. POTIONEERING

The next day at school was fairly uneventful.
Charlie and Sam kept staring suspiciously at
the wannabe POOPers but they never came
near which was definitely a good thing.
Word had obviously started to get round at
break time and, during the lunch hour, there
were some very random questions being
asked like, *Did you really turn the
playground into an outdoor ice-rink?* or, *If
my mum says it's OK, could you magic me a
white rabbit?* and Jamie's personal favourite,

Is it true that you're related to that magician on TV? Secretly, all four children were quite enjoying being the centre of attention and they started to think about what they might do with their next magic potion.

'We could freeze the gravy at lunch time then we wouldn't have to have it all over our sausages,' was Alfie's best suggestion.

'I think we should freeze Mrs Carter when she starts talking about maths. Just until playtime, obviously,' Eve offered hopefully.

'I like maths,' objected Jamie, 'I quite liked the idea of turning the playground into an outdoor ice rink. Then we could all go skating.'

'Maybe we could try making a different type of potion,' suggested Lauren. 'I mean, we know the freezing one works, maybe we could do a shrinking one next.'

'Shrinking sounds a bit tricky,' Jamie frowned, 'but what about a colour changing potion? That might be an option.' Jamie was still a little bit shocked by what had happened the day before. He had really wanted to teach Charlie and Sam a lesson but it had never even occurred to him that the potion might actually work. Neville had pretty much admitted that he had helped but he had also hinted that he thought the children were pretty close to working out how to do it themselves.

'I know what we could do,' Lauren said. 'Remember that jug thing Mum asked Dad to get the other day? It was supposed to be pale green but Dad picked up the wrong box and bought the peach one. We could try to change that. Even if it goes wrong, it's only a jug.'

'Your mum might not be very pleased,' said Eve.

'She'll be delighted, well, she will be if it works.'

'Let's try it,' said Jamie. 'Although, I'm not sure I can remember what we did.'

'Lucky I wrote it down then.' Eve, waved her notebook at him.

'Yeah, lucky,' agreed Lauren. 'You're always in such a hurry to finish everything Jamie. You're lucky to have us girls to do the brain work for you.' Both girls laughed and Jamie scowled at them.

'If you're so good at the brain work, does that mean you've worked out what Neville did to make the freezing potion work? If we can't do that, there's probably not much point even trying another potion.'

The four friends studied the recipe in

Eve's book then gathered up everything they needed. After the basic mixture was made, Alfie had a question.

'What's the magic ingredient this time?'

'What do you mean?' asked Lauren.

'Well, Neville said we were very close to making things work ourselves so it has to be something to do with the magic ingredient. You made a freezing potion by adding an ice pole. What are you planning to use for a colour change?'

'Good point,' said Eve. Lauren nodded her agreement and they both turned to Jamie.

'What are you looking at me for?' Jamie asked.

'Because it was your crazy magic that made everything work the last time,' replied Lauren.

'I have no idea why that happened

yesterday. It must have been something to do with Neville because it certainly wasn't because of anything I did!' protested Jamie.

'Whatever,' said Alfie. 'We still need a plan.' He paused for a moment then grinned. 'I know! What about a chameleon?'

'A chameleon!' exclaimed Eve. 'Even if we knew where to find one, I bet we'd never be able to catch it and, even if we managed that, it would be totally cruel to put one in a potion. We are definitely NOT using a chameleon! Okay?'

'Okay,' Alfie looked hurt. 'I was only trying to help. Nobody else was coming up with anything.'

'We're making it too complicated,' Jamie said. 'We don't need a colour changing ingredient. We just need something green. We're not trying to create a colour changing jug, we just want it to be a green jug. Let's just add some grass.'

They all agreed that, in the absence of a chameleon, grass was a pretty good option. The boys went to collect a supply while the girls smuggled the jug out of the kitchen without being caught. They gathered in front of the summer house ready for the magic to start. Lauren laid the peach jug on the grass and stood back. Jamie held up the pot of basic potion mix in one hand and a bunch of grass in the other. 'Okay, everybody concentrate really hard. We all need to focus on turning the jug green.'

Everyone fell silent, staring at the jug. Suddenly, Alfie's tummy gave a loud grumble.

'Alfie!' the other three all cried out.

'Sorry, I can't help it. I didn't have time

for a snack after school. I'm starving.'

'How can you be thinking about food at a time like this?' asked Eve. 'There's important magic to be done.'

They all focussed on the jug once again until, finally, Jamie dropped the grass into the mixture then quickly poured the potion over the jug. Slowly, very slowly, the jug faded to an interesting shade of yellow then, eventually, pale green. For the second time in two days, the four friends were speechless. The potion had worked again and it gradually began to dawn on them – the possibilities were endless.

4. BIGGER THINGS

'What did your mum say about the jug?' Eve asked Lauren next morning.

'It was so funny,' Lauren giggled. 'She thought Dad had changed it at the shop and she was saying *that's so thoughtful* and thanking him and everything. Dad had no idea what she was talking about but he obviously decided just to go along with it. They were being all lovey-dovey and stuff. Jamie and I could hardly stop laughing.'

'Then, after tea,' Jamie joined in, 'Mum

took the jug out of the cupboard and it had turned back to peach again. Neither of them could believe their eyes!' he laughed.

'Aw, so the potion didn't work.' Eve was clearly disappointed.

'Well, it did work, it just didn't last. I'm not sure what we can do about that.'

After school, the children returned to their summer house laboratory. So far, both the potions they had created had worked and they were all starting to become a bit more ambitious. Alfie, who had to wash both his parents' cars every weekend to earn his pocket money, was keen to develop a cleaning potion to help with that. Jamie felt it was probably too risky to mess with something as expensive as a car until they had done more testing. Lauren pointed out that, even if a potion made the cars clean, it probably wouldn't last anyway and Alfie could get into serious trouble. Eve and Lauren were keen to try to magic up a pony or even just a puppy but they couldn't think what they would add to the mixture to make that happen. Eventually, Jamie took charge.

'Let's make a growing potion and we can use it on the trampoline!'

Eve wasn't sure her friends' huge trampoline needed to be any bigger but Jamie reminded her of his mum's rule that only two people were allowed on at a time. For once, Lauren agreed with her brother, pointing out how much more fun it would be if they could all go on together. The question was, what could they add to the potion to make it grow things?

'Ice makes things freeze. Grass made stuff

green. What makes things grow?' wondered Jamie.

'Horse poo!' shouted Alfie. 'My grandpa puts horse poo in his garden to make stuff grow. He says it's his magic ingredient.'

'And where,' asked Eve, 'do you suggest we get horse poo? You might not have noticed but none of us has a horse.'

'Well, Grandad gets it from the lady up the road. She puts it in plastic bags and he brings them home in the boot of his car.' Alfie explained. 'It does stink a bit though,' he admitted. 'Well, quite a lot really…and we don't have a car. Maybe we need another idea.' Alfie looked sad that his idea was a bit rubbish but, as Lauren pointed out, at least he was trying to think of something. Nobody else had come up with anything better.

'I know,' said Eve, 'I have some of those

little magnifying glasses you get in Christmas crackers. They make things bigger. Why don't we try them?'

They all agreed that was the best plan so Eve went to collect the magnifying glasses while the others gathered up the ingredients and mixed the basic potion once again. Following their previous successes, they were very careful to measure everything out exactly. They didn't want carelessness to mess things up at this stage. Finally, the potion was ready and Eve had returned with the magic ingredient. Jamie handed her the bottle with a very serious expression on his face. This was important to him. He really wanted a bigger trampoline.

Eve held the bottle in one hand and five little magnifying glasses in the other. Like a magician, she slowly brought her hands

together, held the magic ingredients over the bottle and dropped them…onto the ground.

'They won't fit,' she said, unnecessarily. 'Please can I have a bigger tub?'

Finally, with the basic potion in a little blue seaside bucket, Eve added the magnifying glasses then threw the whole mixture over the trampoline.

Nothing happened.

'We really need to concentrate,' Jamie said and they all closed their eyes.

Nothing happened.

'I hate to tell you this, guys but it's not working.' Alfie stated the obvious.

'You don't say!' Eve replied, sarcastically.

'Maybe it's because it wasn't Jamie,' suggested Lauren. 'Maybe the last two worked because it was Jamie that added the special ingredient and threw the potion,'

'Maybe it's Jamie that's magic,' said Alfie. 'That would be amazing!'

'Don't be ridiculous. I mean, he's a pretty good brother most of the time but he's certainly not magic.'

'What do you mean, most of the time?' Jamie pretended to look hurt.

'Come on you two,' said Eve. 'We don't have time for this. Let's make another batch and Jamie can try it then we'll know if that's the problem.'

They set to work again, measuring ingredients and retrieving the magnifying glasses that were lying on the trampoline. They double and triple checked everything, taking no chances. Finally, they were ready for a second attempt. Jamie stepped forward with the bucket and the magnifying glasses.

Secretly, he quite liked the idea that he was the one with the magic and he was really hoping it would work this time. He waited for silence then added the magic ingredient and threw the new potion over the trampoline.

Nothing happened.

Alfie opened his mouth to speak but Jamie held his hand up for silence. They all watched and waited, each imagining themselves on a giant trampoline.

Nothing happened.

Eventually, they all stopped believing that anything was going to happen and, disappointed, they went back to the summer house. As they quietly tidied up their containers and ingredients, they each kept looking over at the trampoline, just in case the effect was delayed and it eventually grew.

But it never did.

5. PRACTICE MAKES PERFECT

They just couldn't figure out what had gone wrong. The recipe had been the same, the magic ingredient made sense and, the second time, the same person had applied the potion.

'There was no reason for it not to work. We did everything right.' Secretly, Jamie was a bit disappointed that he hadn't been able to make the potion work after Eve had failed.

'Maybe it was the magnifying glasses. Maybe they weren't strong enough,' Eve tried.

'Told you we should have used horse poo,' said Alfie, still grumpy. 'Nobody ever listens to my ideas.

'Don't talk rubbish, Alfie, we did listen. It was just a rubbish idea. How would we ever have found horse poo?' Jamie asked.

'Come on you two, it's not worth fighting about. We need to work together if we're ever going to work out what went wrong,' said Lauren.

'Clever girl, you're absolutely right,' said a small voice from above their heads. The children looked up to see Neville perched on the edge of the summer house roof. 'Remember what I said – four brains are far better than one so make sure you use them all! Maybe you should think about the reasons why you used each potion. Maybe that'll help you work out why they didn't work, if you know what I mean. Good luck!' and he disappeared over the roof before anyone else could speak.

At first the children couldn't work out what Neville meant. The three reasons they had used the potions were all different. They had wanted to teach the bullies a lesson, they had wanted to fix Lauren and Jamie's mum's jug and they had wanted to expand the trampoline. All very different. Or were they?

Suddenly Lauren said, 'maybe the potions only work when we're doing something good!'
The others looked at her, confused. 'Think about it,' she continued. 'When we froze the grass, it stopped Charlie and Sam being horrible to us and when we changed the colour of the jug, it made Mum happy. The

potions only work to make good things happen.'

'But making the trampoline bigger was something good,' Jamie said, 'and that didn't work.'

'But that was just for ourselves,' explained Lauren. 'We weren't doing something kind for someone else that time. I think the magic only works when we use it for good reasons.'

The others agreed that Lauren might be onto something and they decided to test the theory. It was difficult to use the freezing potion again because Charlie and Sam had been so scared the first time that they hadn't given them any trouble since. The other option was the jug but both Lauren and Jamie thought changing that again might send their mum into orbit and that definitely didn't count as a good thing. Surprisingly, it was Alfie that eventually had a brainwave.

'My grandpa, you know, the one with the horse poo? Well, his next-door neighbour, Joe, is always asking to borrow tools and stuff but Grandpa gets cross because, quite often, Joe gives them back broken and he never offers to pay to get them fixed. Grandpa doesn't want to sound like a bad neighbour by telling Joe he can't borrow stuff but he's fed up of having to buy new tools all the time.'

'That's all very interesting, Alfie but what does it have to do with our potions?' asked Jamie.

'Hang on a minute, I'm coming to that. This morning, Joe asked if he could borrow Grandpa's lawnmower because his is away to be repaired. Grandpa *really* doesn't want to

lend it. If we could come up with a potion that temporarily broke Grandpa's lawnmower, just before Joe borrowed it, Joe might think it was rubbish and stop asking for other stuff in future.'

'So, you're saying that breaking your grandpa's lawnmower would be a good thing,' said Eve.

'Yes…just as long as it was only temporary.'

Everyone fell silent. They were each thinking through the idea of temporarily breaking Alfie's grandpa's lawnmower. The main issue was that Alfie's grandpa lived too far away for them to walk to his house. Not only that but, even if they could come up with a magic breaking ingredient, a lawnmower is quite an expensive item to be messing around with. Thirdly, although previous potions had only worked temporarily, that hadn't really been planned so nobody could guarantee what might happen this time. They were a brave bunch though and they knew that the only way they would ever perfect their potions was to keep trying them out. Jamie and Lauren went to ask their mum if she would take them all to Alfie's grandpa's house so that they could help him tidy up his garden. She hadn't been convinced at first but they'd managed to persuade her to check with Eve's and Alfie's parents and, eventually, it was all agreed. She dropped them off at Grandpa's with their potion kit and the usual request for them to be good. She told them she'd be back in an hour so they didn't have much time. Grandpa was a bit surprised to see them all but said he was glad to have some company while he was working in his garden. Alfie asked him about the lawnmower and if he was going to lend it to Joe.

'I don't really have much option, Alfie, Joe's a good neighbour most of the time. I don't want to get in his bad books by not lending him a mower when he's desperate. He'll be round for it shortly.'

'We can get it out of the shed for you if you want,' offered Alfie.

'Go on then, good lad.'

Alfie led the others round the back of the house to the garden shed. They knew they would have to be quick and they still didn't have their magic ingredient. While the boys were bringing the mower out of the shed, the girls mixed the basic potion. Suddenly, Alfie cried out, 'I know! We could use a stone!'

The others looked puzzled so he

explained. 'Stones always break lawnmowers. It happens all the time when Grandpa's not paying attention. If we put a stone in the potion, that might do the trick.'

Nobody had any better ideas so they agreed it was worth a try. Alfie took a stone from the path which they added to the basic potion before throwing the whole lot over the mower. Before they had time to do anything else, Grandpa appeared round the side of the house with Joe.

'Hi Alfie, I haven't seen you for ages. You're fairly growing up. I see you've got the lawnmower all ready for me. Thanks.'

'Erm…yeah…no problem,' mumbled Alfie, not sure what else to say.

'Why is it all wet?' Grandpa asked.

'Erm…Jamie was having a drink and he accidentally spilled some. It's just water though. It'll be okay.'

'Sorry,' Jamie looked just that. He was a bit miffed that Alfie had chosen him to take the blame but he didn't want to give the game away so he didn't say anything else.

'Never mind, I'm sure it'll be fine. Thanks very much George, much appreciated. I'll bring it back later on.' Joe wheeled the lawnmower away.

Alfie's grandpa looked at the children. 'Is there anything you want to tell me?' he asked. 'You all look very guilty. Should I be worried?'

'No Grandpa, it's fine. Sorry about the water. We were messing about and it just got knocked out of Jamie's hand.'

'Oh well, no harm done. Why don't you all come and help me finish my weeding then I'll see if I can find some biscuits.'

They were halfway through the custard creams when Lauren and Jamie's mum arrived to pick them up…just at the same time as Joe was getting ready to cut his grass next door. As the children were getting into the car, they heard Joe trying to start the mower. Then they heard him calling out to Alfie's grandpa. The four friends all looked at each other. It sounded as though the potion had worked. What mattered now was how temporary it would be. Unfortunately, the car pulled away before they could find out what the problem was and the worried children could only wave to Alfie's grandpa as they drove off down the street. They were going to have to wait to find out the full extent of the damage.

6. SUPERHEROES?

Next morning, Alfie greeted Lauren and Jamie with a huge grin. 'Good morning fellow super heroes! Is it today we're taking over the world?'

Jamie laughed. 'Does that mean it worked?'

'Like a dream! Grandpa was telling Mum all about it. Apparently, the mower wouldn't work for Joe so he brought it back. By the time Grandpa tried it, everything was fine but Joe said it didn't matter any more because his lawnmower was fixed and ready to be collected.'

'So, the potion worked, your grandpa doesn't have to lend his lawnmower to Joe and they haven't fallen out. Perfect!'

'Yip!' said Alfie. 'So…world domination…what do you think the magic ingredient is for that?'

'We're hardly at that stage, Alfie. We need to come up with a few more good deeds first,' Lauren pointed out.

'Then can we take over the world? Please?' Alfie was not going to be easily put off.

Just then Eve arrived and she did not look happy at all. Lauren asked her what was wrong and Eve blurted out, 'Amber was bullied yesterday!' Amber was Eve's little sister. She was five and had only been at school for a few weeks. 'Those big girls, Emmy and Paige caught her at break time and made her give them her crisps.'

'That's awful!' Lauren was horrified. 'They can't do that to a little kid.'

'I don't think that's the first time either,' Eve continued. 'Amber says it's happened to some of her friends too.'

The bell rang and the four friends had to go to their classroom but they spent the morning thinking about Amber and her friends. They finally had the chance to talk about it at break time.

'We need to take on those bullies and tell them to stop picking on people.' Alfie was clearly still in super-hero mode.

'Take it easy Alfie,' cautioned Jamie. 'You're right, we should do something but let's be clever about it and not just charge in with our capes on!'

Alfie looked disappointed. 'What do you mean?' he asked.

'Well, first of all, let's go and see exactly what these bullies are up to.'

Jamie and Alfie quietly searched the playground until they spotted Emmy and Paige. Sure enough, the two older girls had cornered one of the little ones and appeared to be making some sort of demand. Thinking quickly, the two boys pretended they were chasing each other and Alfie 'accidentally' ended up in the corner.

'Get lost loser!' snapped Paige. 'You shouldn't be round here.' She turned to face Alfie, trying to block his view of what was going on.

Alfie wanted to run. Paige was two years older than him and *loads* taller. He

concentrated really hard on not backing away. You should never show a bully that you're scared. He remembered how upset Eve had been that morning about what had happened to her little sister then he remembered how much he wanted to be a super-hero.

'Sorry,' Alfie said to Paige, craning his neck so that he could look her straight in the eye. He thought fast. 'We were just playing tag…oh, hi Maisie!' he called past Paige, recognising the little girl that she and Emmy had cornered. 'Are you enjoying being at school?' Alfie was delighted when the little girl burst into tears. Well, he was sorry she was upset but it made carrying out the rest of his plan so much easier. 'Oh no! Are things not going very well?' he asked her then continued without giving her any chance to reply, 'come on, come with me. I know exactly who you need to speak to.' Alfie held his hand out to Maisie who took it and held on tightly. 'Don't worry girls, I'll take it from here.' Alfie grinned at Emmy and Paige who could only watch in stunned silence as he led the little girl away.

Alfie and Jamie promised Maisie that they would sort out the bullies then they delivered her safely to a teacher before heading back to class. Now, they were even more certain that they had to do something. They discussed the options with the girls. They knew they could use a potion because they were doing something good for someone else. They also knew that Paige and Emmy were a far bigger challenge than Charlie and Sam had been. The boys could be a pain and make life a bit uncomfortable at times but the girls were nasty. They didn't stop until they got what they wanted, no matter who they hurt in the process. The girls were proper bullies.

The four friends arranged to meet at the potion factory after school to decide what to do.

7. THE NEXT CHALLENGE

'OK, no pressure but this has to be our best potion ever.' Alfie was still upset about Maisie.

'We've got to stop those two from bullying anyone else.' Eve was still upset about Amber.

'Yeah well, we already know all that. What do you suggest we actually do?' Jamie was just a little bit upset that he didn't seem to be in charge any more. He'd done all the hard work to create the potion in the first place. Now it felt like everyone else was telling him what to do.

As usual, Lauren was the peacemaker. 'I suggest we all work together on some sort of potion that lets us show Emmy and Paige that they can't get away with being nasty any more. We need to do it in secret so that nobody knows we're involved and we need to make sure none of the little ones are caught up in the magic.'

'That sounds like a very big challenge,' said Eve. 'Do you really think we can do it?'

'Of course we can.' Jamie took charge again. 'And I think I know how.' Suddenly he had their attention again. 'We make ourselves invisible'

'Wow!' exclaimed Alfie. 'That'll be amazing. I've always wanted to be invisible. What do I have to do?'

Jamie had absolutely no idea how they could make themselves invisible but he wasn't about to admit that. 'It's quite straightforward,' he said, importantly, pausing to give himself time to think. 'We make the same basic potion that we've used before and have it ready for when we see Paige and Emmy starting their trouble. We'll be hiding nearby so no-one sees the potion taking effect. We make ourselves invisible then we can go right up to the bullies and use whatever tricks we can think of to scare them away.'

'Brilliant!' Alfie was impressed.

'Let's get mixing,' Eve was keen to get started.

'Just one question,' said Lauren, 'what's our magic ingredient?'

Jamie had been hoping the others

wouldn't notice that he'd skipped that part. Trust his sister to catch him out. 'For goodness' sake,' he said, 'do I have to come up with all the good ideas?'

'No,' said Lauren, 'but one of us has to come up with that one or there's no point in us even starting on another potion.'

Jamie knew Lauren was right but he'd considered everything and he just couldn't come up with anything that might work as an invisibility ingredient. Surely they weren't going to fail at this point. They were so close to success, Jamie could almost taste it. Oh, and he wanted to help the younger kids too, of course.

'The only slightly invisible thing I have is the ink in my spy-pen.' Eve was thinking aloud. 'But there wouldn't be enough of that.'

'Mum has that invisible thread she uses for delicate stuff,' added Lauren. 'She wouldn't be very happy if we took that though.'

'We're making it too complicated again,' said Alfie with a sudden grin. The others all looked at him. 'We don't need something invisible, we need something transparent.' His friends looked puzzled. 'It means see-through. We need to make ourselves see-through!' Alfie exclaimed

'Yes!' came a triumphant, high-pitched squeak from above. The children all looked up to see Professor Mixer sitting on the roof. 'Sorry,' he whispered, clasping his hand over his mouth. 'You're just brilliant - all of you. You're working so hard and co-operating so well with each other. It's just brilliant.'

'I thought you weren't allowed to help

us,' said Eve.

'I'm not helping you,' the professor replied. 'It's just that you four are by far the most exciting prospects POOP has at the moment and I'm desperate for you to succeed. I just can't stay away.'

'Do you think Alfie's right then?' Jamie was keen to make use of the expert knowledge. 'Do you think transparent is the way to go – not invisible?'

'It's really not my place to say,' Professor Mixer saw the disappointment on the children's faces. He looked around to make sure no-one was watching then he leaned towards them. 'It's got to be worth a try though, right?' With that, the little pink man winked at them then disappeared up over the roof of the summer house.

'Aaargh!' Jamie snarled in exasperation.

'I wish he would stop just popping in with half a story then vanishing before we work out the rest. It doesn't help.'

'Yes it does,' argued Lauren. 'He said we're working well and that Alfie's idea's worth a try. What we need to do now is find something transparent and test the spell on something unimportant.'

'Unimportant?' asked Alfie.

'Yes, like a stick or an old toy or something,' explained Lauren. She saw Alfie was still confused and continued more slowly. 'Something that's not a human being just in case the spell works but doesn't wear off again. I don't know about you but I don't want to be see-through for the rest of my life. That would just be awkward.'

'Good point,' agreed Alfie.

'Never mind all that,' grumbled Jamie.

'None of this even matters unless we can find something transparent to use as our magic ingredient. The only thing I can think of is glass but that would be a really bad idea.'

'Why is it a bad idea?' asked Alfie. 'You don't get anything more see-through than glass. It would be perfect.'

'Yeah, perfect,' agreed Jamie sarcastically, 'until we throw the potion over someone and cut them to pieces.'

'Oh yeah. I didn't think about that.'

'I might have an alternative,' Eve sounded a bit unsure. 'My mum has loads of those plastic file things, you know, for putting paper into when you want it in a folder?' I could easily get some of those and we could chop them up to whatever size we wanted. The bits would mix into the potion and they wouldn't hurt anyone.' She stopped when she saw Jamie's grumpy face. He clearly wasn't impressed.

'I think it's a great idea,' Lauren said quickly before her brother could argue. 'Let's try it. We need more ingredients for the basic potion too so we'd better get a move on.'

It didn't take long for the potioneers to collect everything they needed and prepare the basic potion mix. They'd done it so many times now they hardly even needed their recipe. While the boys worked on that, Eve went home to collect the plastic files and Lauren found scissors so they could chop the files into little pieces. Soon, everything was ready. Following Lauren's earlier comments, they agreed to test this potion on a large stone in the garden. 'It's nice and solid,' said Jamie. 'If we can make that invisible, we can easily do it to one of us.'

The four friends were very excited as they stood around the stone.

'This is our most important potion yet,' said Lauren, gravely.

'It could change everything,' added Eve.

'It could turn us into super-heroes!' squealed Alfie excitedly. The others glared at him. 'Sorry, sorry,' he said and quietened down.

'OK,' Jamie took charge again. 'We should time this to see how long the stone stays invisible for. That might be important when we use it for real.'

'Good idea – I'll do it,' volunteered Eve, always keen to show off her new watch.

'Ready?' asked Jamie. Everyone nodded, holding their breath in anticipation.

Jamie held the potion out in front of him, dropped in a handful of chopped up plastic file then poured the whole lot over the stone.

It completely disappeared.

'Wow!' breathed Alfie.

'It worked,' Lauren was amazed.

Eve was a bit distracted by the time-keeping but the other three got down onto their hands and knees and looked through the space where the stone had been.

'It's completely disappeared,' muttered Jamie, holding out his hand, 'but I can still feel it.' The others all reached out to touch the space.

'Absolutely brilliant!' exclaimed Alfie. 'We're geniuses!'

They stayed sitting on the ground, marvelling at their own brilliance and continuing to watch the space.

Unsurprisingly, Alfie was the first to get bored. 'It's taking ages. Do you think it's not

going to come back?'

'Seven minutes,' said Eve, never taking her eyes off her watch.

'We'll need at least that to sort out Emmy and Paige,' said Jamie. 'We don't want it wearing off too soon.'

'We do want it to wear off at some point though,' Lauren pointed out.

They waited a little longer, watching the space, until the grey of the stone started to reappear.

'Nine minutes, 24 seconds,' said Eve. 'Is that long enough?'

'I guess it'll have to be,' replied Jamie.

'The real question is – which one of us gets to try it tomorrow?' asked Alfie. 'I'd really, really like it to be me.' He turned towards Jamie, showing his big, pleading eyes.

'I think I'd like to have a go too,' said Eve. 'What about you two?' She turned to Jamie and Lauren.

'I'm not that bothered,' Lauren didn't want to admit it but she felt a little bit scared, not just of the bullies but also of being made invisible. She still worried that the potion might not wear off.

Jamie shrugged. 'I'm not that bothered either.' He felt a bit scared too but he would definitely never admit it. 'I should probably be in charge of applying the potion anyway as I've got the most experience of that,' he added importantly. Alfie and Eve knew that meant Jamie was scared but, because they both wanted to be invisible, neither of them said anything.

It was agreed that they would look for their chance the following day at break. Alfie and Eve would both be made invisible whilst Jamie and Lauren hid nearby to make sure everything went smoothly.

All they needed now was for their plan to work.

8. TAKING ON THE BULLIES

Alfie and Eve were waiting at the school gates when Jamie and Lauren arrived the following morning.

'Have you brought the potion?' Alfie asked.

'Nah, I decided not to bother today,' Jamie replied, sarcastically.

'Just ignore him, Alfie,' advised Lauren. 'He didn't get enough sleep last night and he's *really* grumpy.'

'I didn't get enough sleep because I was

thinking through all the stuff we've got to do today. The magic doesn't happen by itself you know. Somebody has to take responsibility. Although I don't understand why it always has to be me.' Jamie grumbled, proving his sister right.

'That is *so* unfair, Jamie!' Now it was Eve's turn to be cross. 'We've all worked really hard at this and we all know exactly what we're supposed to do. You shouldn't keep taking over if you don't want the responsibility!'

'Stop! Both of you! This isn't helping anyone,' said Lauren as the bell rang signalling the start of school. We all need to calm down and keep quiet until break time or people will be suspicious. Let's meet round the back near the bins. Nobody ever goes there.'

The morning dragged and the four friends were very distracted. Jamie forgot what six times eight was and was very embarrassed when Lauren had to remind him. Eve forgot to change her shoes and made muddy footprints all over the carpet. Alfie completely forgot where he was and called the teacher 'Mum', much to the amusement of his classmates. Eventually, break time arrived and the hopeful potioneers managed to sneak away to the far corner of the playground without being seen. They were all very nervous.

'What if it doesn't work?' asked Eve.

'That would probably be better than it starting to work then something going wrong,' said Lauren. 'We could get into all sorts of trouble.'

'It's going to be fine.' Jamie was optimistic. 'We know exactly what we have to do. All we need now is to catch those bullies getting up to their tricks.'

'Well, stand by because there they are.' Alfie was first to spot Paige and Emmy and they were steering a much smaller girl away from the safety of all her friends.

'OK, here goes. The potion's ready to go as soon as you two are,' Jamie said.

Alfie and Eve looked at each other then gripped hands. 'Ready,' they both said at the same time. Nobody spoke as Lauren passed the magic ingredient to her brother. Jamie added it to the basic potion and threw the whole lot over Eve and Alfie. They immediately disappeared.

'It didn't work,' Alfie was disappointed.

'Oh yes it did!' Jamie replied, 'you've gone!'

'You'd better get over there,' prompted Lauren. 'You have less than ten minutes before it wears off.'

'Oh no!' said Eve. 'I forgot to give you my watch. It's invisible now. How will we time it?'

'I guess we can't,' said Jamie. 'Just don't waste any time. Get back here as soon as you can.'

'Now go,' urged Lauren. 'We'll watch you from here.'

Although Lauren and Jamie couldn't see their friends, they knew when they reached their target because Paige's arm suddenly went straight up in the air.

'What are you doing?' Emmy snapped. 'Stop messing about!' Emmy turned back to the frightened little girl in front of her. 'Now, as I was saying, I don't ever want to…'

Emmy stopped talking in disbelief. Her own left hand was moving up in front of her face and, before she could do anything, it slapped her across the cheek. Paige tried to stop herself from laughing but when Emmy's ponytail suddenly started twirling all by itself, she couldn't help it. Emmy was really cross with her friend. 'What are you doing, Paige? Cut it out. It's not funny!'

'I'm not doing anything,' Paige protested. 'I'm not even touching you. Why are you doing all that crazy stuff?'

'I'm not!' Emmy was getting really angry. 'Now stop being weird and help me.' She had just noticed her shoelaces had come undone then tied themselves together so she couldn't walk.

Alfie and Eve were really enjoying themselves, each trying to come up with a better trick than the previous one. Unfortunately, they completely lost track of the time. Lauren and Jamie were watching from behind the bins when Lauren suddenly realised they had a problem. 'Jamie, look! Alfie's feet are starting to reappear! We've got to get them out of there!'

'Oh no! That's not part of the plan. The potion must be wearing off. What can we do?'

'We should have kept some of the potion in reserve. In case of emergency.'

'I did! But we'll never get close enough to put it on them without getting caught.'

'It's not for them, silly, it's for me. I'm going in to rescue them!'

Jamie finally caught up with his sister's

plan and pulled the reserve potion out of his bag along with the chopped up files. He quickly mixed the two and poured them over Lauren who immediately disappeared.

By the time Lauren joined the others, Eve had realised there was a problem and was trying to let Alfie know. Unfortunately, he was so busy making Paige and Emmy poke each other and hit themselves in the face, he hadn't noticed the nudges. When Lauren was close enough, she nipped him hard on the arm, making him squeal. Everyone froze.

'What on earth was that?' Emmy's voice was shaky. 'I don't know what's going on here but I don't like it. We need to get out of here.'

Alfie had taken the chance to get his reappearing feet out of the way so it was left up to Lauren and Eve to finish the job they had started. Lauren grabbed Emmy under the arms, Eve picked up her feet and they laid her down on the ground. Before she could do anything, they did the same with Paige, putting her beside her friend with their feet together. As a finishing touch, Lauren knotted all their shoe laces together as tightly as she could.

By the time the bell rang for the end of morning break, Eve was starting to reappear and Lauren was hiding behind the dustbins waiting to do the same. Thankfully, Alfie seemed to be completely back to normal as he rescued the little girl that Paige and Emmy had been bullying and took her back to her teacher. Jamie was pleased that their plan seemed to have worked although he was a little bit sad that he was the only one that hadn't been invisible. Maybe he would get a chance another time.

9. PROFESSOR MIXER RETURNS

When Jamie, Alfie and Eve finally made it
back to the classroom, they found Paige and
Emmy being comforted by Mrs Carter. Both
girls were crying and rambling on about
twirling ponytails and shoes that tied
themselves together. The teacher clearly
thought they were hallucinating and she was
making them sip water before sitting down
with their heads between their knees.
Eventually, she sent one of the other children
to fetch a first-aider. The main advantage of

all the drama was that Lauren, who had been waiting to become visible again, was able to sneak back into the class without being seen!

'Are they OK?' she asked Eve.

'They will be and I think it's safe to say they won't be bothering the little ones any more. I heard Emmy telling Mrs C that she was sorry for all the bad stuff she's done. Mrs C just thinks she has a fever.'

'I was worried they might not realise all the crazy stuff was happening because of what they were doing.'

'I think they got the message loud and clear. When I was running away I heard Paige telling Emmy that she had known something bad would happen if they kept picking on the little kids.'

Alfie was reflecting on their success too. 'Super-hero status for us now! We were amazing!'

'We were,' replied Jamie, 'but you do realise that nobody else can ever know? We can't ever tell anyone about what we did. It could cause all sorts of problems if people start expecting us to be able to make ourselves invisible and sort things out for them and stuff.'

'I hadn't thought about that,' said Alfie, sadly. 'I was really looking forward to being everyone's hero for a while. Could I not just tell one person, Grandpa maybe?'

'No way! I mean it, Alfie. You mustn't ever tell anyone about any of this. You just have to feel good knowing that you did it and stopped those two from bullying anyone else.'

All was not lost though as the children found out after school. They were in the summer house in Lauren and Jamie's garden, reliving the day's events - how ridiculous Paige and Emmy had looked when their arms and hair were doing crazy things, how scared Lauren had felt when she saw Alfie's feet reappearing before they should have and how Mrs Carter had thought the girls were making everything up to get out of class for a while! Suddenly, there was a funny, rumbling noise from the roof. Jamie was first out of the door to see what was happening, closely followed by his friends. They all gaped, open-mouthed when they saw what was on the summer house roof – dozens of tiny people, all dressed in different colours. At the very front, resplendent in pink, stood Professor Mixer. When he saw the children, he held up his hand to silence the tiny crowd then cleared his throat and began to speak.

'My fellow potioneers, as you are aware, it has been some time since we uncovered fantastic new talent in our line of work but I believe that day has come at last. The four people you see before you have been working very hard to perfect their potioneering expertise and finally, today, they have achieved convincing success. They have pulled together as a strong team and discovered that potions are not for the faint-hearted. They have shown dedication and commitment to our cause and, ultimately, learned that potioneering can only ever be successful when it is being used to achieve good things. I believe that all of these things mean they should immediately be promoted to Party POOPers. Ladies and gentlemen, please show your appreciation for Jamie, Lauren, Eve and Alfie!'

The crowd went wild! The tiny people were clapping and cheering, twirling each other around and waving their arms in the air. As the celebrations subsided, they started chanting the children's names, dancing from one foot to the other. Finally, Alfie knew what it was like to be a hero!

'This is awesome!' he yelled to the others. 'I love it!'

'I hope Mum can't hear,' Lauren whispered to Jamie. 'She'll be worried about what the neighbours think.'

'I'm still not sure I want to be a POOPer,' Eve said. 'It doesn't sound very nice.'

'I think we're supposed to be honoured,' Jamie whispered. 'Just smile and go with it for now. We can work out the details later.'

The 'details' turned out to be an awards ceremony, run by Professor Mixer. All the children were given a tiny certificate and a medal shaped like a potions bottle. The professor made yet another speech and his friends clapped and cheered all over again. Finally, the festivities were brought to a close by Jamie and Lauren's mum calling them in for tea. As quickly as they had arrived, all the tiny potioneers disappeared back to wherever it was they had come from.

Professor Mixer was the last to leave, calling ominously over his shoulder, 'Well done again. I'll be in touch when we need you!'

MESSAGE FROM THE AUTHOR

Thank you so much for reading my book. I hope you enjoyed it and I hope, when you mix potions, they turn out to be magic too!

Happy reading,

Jill x

Printed in Poland
by Amazon Fulfillment
Poland Sp. z o.o., Wrocław

51944591R00063